The Mozart Question

The Mozart Question

Michael Morpurgo

illustrated by
Michael Foreman

WALKER
BOOKS

First published 2006 in *Singing for Mrs Pettigrew:
A Story-maker's Journey* by Walker Books Ltd,
87 Vauxhall Walk, London SE11 5HJ

This edition published 2015

4 6 8 10 9 7 5 3

Text © 2006 Michael Morpurgo
Illustrations © 2007 Michael Foreman

The right of Michael Morpurgo and Michael Foreman to be identified
as author and illustrator respectively of this work has been asserted by them
in accordance with the Copyright, Designs and Patents Act 1988

This book has been typeset in Adobe Caslon

Printed and bound in Great Britain by Clays Ltd, St Ives plc

British Library Cataloguing in Publication Data:
a catalogue record for this book is available from the British Library

ISBN 978-1-4063-6639-6

www.walker.co.uk

For Christine Baker

M.M. & M.F.

The question I am most often asked is always easy enough to answer. Question: how did you get started as a writer? Answer: funnily enough, by asking someone almost exactly that very same question, which I was only able to ask in the first place by a dose of extraordinarily good fortune.

I had better explain.

My good fortune was, of course, someone else's rotten luck – it is often that way, I find. The phone call sounded distraught. It came on a Sunday evening. I had only been working on the paper for three weeks. I was a cub reporter, this my first paid job.

"Lesley?" It was my boss, chief arts correspondent Meryl Monkton, a lady not to be messed with. She did not waste time with niceties; she never did. "Listen, Lesley, I have a problem. I was due to go to Venice tomorrow to interview Paolo Levi."

"Paolo Levi?" I said. "The violinist?"

"Is there any other Paolo Levi?" She did not trouble to hide her irritation. "Now look,

Lesley. I've had an accident, a skiing accident, and I'm stuck in hospital in Switzerland. You'll have to go to Venice instead of me."

"Oh, that's terrible," I said, smothering as best I could the excitement surging inside me. Three weeks into the job and I'd be interviewing the great Paolo Levi, and in Venice!

Talk about her accident, I told myself. Sound concerned. Sound very concerned.

"How did it happen?" I asked. "The skiing accident, I mean."

"Skiing," she snapped. "If there's one thing I can't abide, Lesley, it's people feeling sorry for me."

"Sorry," I said.

"I would postpone it if I could, Lesley," she went on, "but I just don't dare. It's taken me more than a year to persuade him to do it. It'll be his first interview in years. And even then I had to agree not to ask him the Mozart question. So don't ask him the Mozart question, is that clear?

If you do he'll like as not cancel the whole interview – he's done it before. We're really lucky to get him, Lesley. I only wish I could be there to do it myself. But you'll have to do."

"The Mozart question?" I asked, rather tentatively.

The silence at the end of the phone was long.

"You mean to say you don't know about Paolo Levi and the Mozart question? Where have you been, girl? Don't you know anything at all about Paolo Levi?"

I suddenly felt I might lose the opportunity altogether if I did not immediately sound informed, and well informed too.

"Well, he would have been born sometime in the mid-1950s," I began. "He must be about fifty by now."

"Exactly fifty in two weeks' time," Meryl Monkton interrupted wearily. "His London concert is his fiftieth birthday concert. That's the whole point of the interview. Go on."

I rattled off all I knew. "Child prodigy and genius, like Yehudi Menuhin. Played his first major concert when he was thirteen. Probably best known for his playing of Bach and Vivaldi. Like Menuhin he played often with Grappelli, equally at home with jazz or Scottish fiddle music or Beethoven. Has played in practically every major concert hall in the world, in front of presidents and kings and queens. I heard him at the Royal Festival Hall in London, five years ago, I think. He was playing Beethoven's Violin Concerto; he was wonderful. Doesn't like applause. Never waits for applause. Doesn't believe in it, apparently. The night I saw him he just walked off the stage and didn't come back. He thinks it's the music that should be applauded if anything, or perhaps the composer, but certainly not the musician. Says that the silence after the performance is part of the music and should not be interrupted. Doesn't record either. Believes music should be live, not canned. Protects his privacy fiercely. Solitary.

Reticent. Lives alone in Venice, where he was
born. Just about the most famous musician
on the planet, and——"

"*The* most famous, Lesley, but he hates obsequiousness. He likes to be talked to straight. So no bowing or scraping, no wide-eyed wonder, and above all no nerves. Can you do that?"

"Yes, Meryl," I replied, knowing only too well that I would have the greatest difficulty even finding my voice in front of the great man.

"And whatever you do, stick to the music. He'll talk till the cows come home about music and composers. But no personal stuff. And above all, keep off the Mozart question. Oh yes, and don't take a tape recorder with you. He hates gadgets. Only shorthand. You can do shorthand, I suppose? Three thousand words. It's your big chance, so don't mess it up, Lesley."

No pressure, then, I thought.

So there I was the next evening outside Paolo Levi's apartment in the Dorsoduro in Venice, on the dot of six o'clock, my throat dry, my heart pounding, trying all I could to compose myself. It occurred to me again, as it had often on the plane, that I still had no idea what this Mozart question was, only

that I mustn't ask it. It was cold, the kind
of cruel chill that seeps instantly into your
bones, deep into your kidneys, and makes
your ears ache. This didn't seem to bother
the street performers in the square behind
me: several grotesquely masked figures on
stilts strutting across the square, an entirely
silver statue-man posing immobile outside

the café with a gaggle of tourists gazing wonderingly at him.

The door opened, and there he was in front of me, Paolo Levi, neat, trim, his famous hair long to his shoulders and jet black.

"I'm Lesley McInley," I said. "I've come from London."

"From the newspaper, I suppose." There was no welcoming smile. "You'd better come in. Shut the door behind you; I hate the cold." His English was perfect, not a trace of an accent. He seemed to be able to follow my thoughts. "I speak English quite well," he said as we went up the stairs. "Language is like music. You learn it best through listening."

He led me down a hallway and into a large room, empty except for a couch by the window piled high with cushions at one end, a grand piano in the centre and a music stand near by. At the other end were just two armchairs and a table. Nothing else. "I like to keep it empty," he said.

It was uncanny. He *was* reading my thoughts. Now I felt even more unnerved.

"Sound needs space to breathe, just the same as we need air," he said.

He waved me to a chair and sat down. "You'll have some mint tea?" he said, pouring me a cup. His dark blue cardigan and grey corduroy trousers were somehow both

shabby and elegant at the same time. The
bedroom slippers he wore looked incongruous
but comfortable. "My feet, they hate the cold
more than the rest of me." He was scrutinizing

me now, his eyes sharp and shining. "You're younger than I expected," he said. "Twenty-three?" He didn't wait to have his estimate confirmed – he knew he was right and he was. "You have heard me play?"

"Beethoven's Violin Concerto. The Royal Festival Hall in London, a few years ago. I was a student." I noticed his violin then, and his bow, on the window ledge.

"I like to practise by the window," he said, "so I can watch the world go by on the canal. It passes the time. Even as a child I never liked practising much. And I love to be near water, to look out on it. When I go to London I have to have a room by the Thames. In Paris I must be by the Seine. I love the light that water makes." He sipped his mint tea, his eyes never leaving me. "Shouldn't you be asking me questions?" He went on. "I'm talking too much. Journalists always make me nervous. I talk too much when I'm nervous. When I go to the dentist's I talk. Before a concert I talk. So let's get this over with, shall we? And not too many questions, please. Why don't we keep it simple? You ask me one question and then let me ramble on. Shall we try that?" I didn't feel at all that he was being dismissive or patronizing, just straight. That didn't make it any easier, though.

I had done my research, made pages of notes, prepared dozens of questions; but now, under his expectant gaze, I simply could not gather my thoughts.

"Well, I know I can't ask you the Mozart question, Signor Levi," I began, "because I've been told not to. I don't even know what the Mozart question is, so I couldn't ask it even if I wanted to; and anyway, I know you don't like it, so I won't."

With every blundering word I was digging myself into a deeper hole. In my desperation I blurted out the first question that came into my head.

"Signor Levi," I said, "I wonder if you'd mind telling me how you got started. I mean, what made you pick up a violin and play that first time?" It was such an obvious question, and personal, too, just the kind of question I shouldn't have asked.

His reaction only confirmed that. He sat back in his chair and closed his eyes. For fully a couple of minutes he said nothing. I was quite sure he was trying to control his impatience, his rage even, that he was going to open his eyes and ask me to leave at once. When he did open his eyes he simply stared up at the ceiling for a while. I could see from the seriousness of his whole demeanour that he was making a decision, and I feared the worst. But instead of throwing me out he stood up and walked slowly to the couch by the window. He picked up his violin and sat back on the cushions with his violin resting on his drawn-up knees. He plucked a string or two and tuned it.

"I will tell you a story," he began. "After it is over you will need to ask me no more questions. Someone once told me that all secrets are lies. The time has come, I think, not to lie any more."

He paused. I felt he was stiffening his resolve, gathering his strength.

"I will start with my father. Papa was a barber. He kept a little barber's shop just behind the Accademia, near the bridge, two minutes from here. We lived above the shop, Mama, Papa and I, but I spent most of my time downstairs in the barber's shop, sitting on the chairs and swinging my legs, smiling at him and his customers in the mirror, and just watching him. I loved those days. I loved him. At the time of these memories I must have been about nine years old. Small for my age. I always was. I still am."

He spoke slowly, very deliberately, as if he was living it again, seeing again everything he was telling me. My shorthand was quick and automatic, so I had time to look up at him occasionally as he spoke. I sensed right away that I was the first person ever to hear this story, so I knew even as he told it just how momentous the telling of it was for him, as in a different way it was for me, too.

"Papa was infinitely deft with his fingers, his scissors playing a constantly changing tune. It seemed to me like a new improvisation

for every customer, the snipping unhesitatingly skilful, so fast it was mesmerizing. He would work always in complete silence, conducting the music of his scissors with his comb. His customers knew better than to interrupt the performance, and so did I. I think perhaps I must have known his customers almost as well as he did. I grew up with them. They were all regulars. Some would close their eyes as Papa worked his magic; others would look back in the mirror at me and wink.

"Shaving was just as fascinating to me, just as rhythmical, too: the swift sweep and dab of the brush, the swish and slap of the razor as Papa sharpened it on the strap, then each time the miraculous unmasking as he stroked

the foam away to reveal a recognizable face

once more.

"After it was all over, he and his customers did talk, and all the banter amongst them was about football, Inter Milan in particular, or sometimes the machinations of politicians and women. What they said I cannot exactly remember, probably because I couldn't understand most of it, but I do know they laughed a lot. I do remember that. Then the next customer would take his seat and a new silence would descend before the performance started and the music of the scissors began. I am sure I first learnt about rhythm in that barber's shop, and about concentration. I learnt to listen, too.

"Papa wasn't just the best barber in all

of Venice – everyone said that – he was a musician, too, a violinist. But strangely he was a violinist who never played the violin. I never heard him play, not once. I only knew he was a violinist because Mama had told me so. She had tears in her eyes whenever she told me about it. That surprised me because she was not a crying woman. He had been so brilliant as a violinist, the best in the whole orchestra, she said. When I asked why he didn't play any more, she turned away from me, went very quiet and told me I'd have to ask Papa myself. So I did. I asked him time and again, and each time he would simply shrug, and say something meaningless like:

'People change, Paolo. Times change.' And that would be that.

"Papa was never a great talker at the best of times, even at home, but I could tell that in this case he was hiding something, that he found my questions both irksome and intrusive. That didn't stop me. I kept on at him. Every time he refused to talk about it I became more suspicious, more sure he had something to hide. It was a child's intuition, I suppose. I sensed a deep secret, but I also sensed after a while that Papa was quite unmovable, that if I was ever going to unlock the secret it would be Mama who would tell me.

"As it turned out, my instinct was right. In the end my almost perpetual pestering proved fruitful, and Mama capitulated – but not in a way I had expected. 'All right, Paolo,' she said after I'd been nagging her about it unmercifully one morning. 'If I show you the violin will you promise me you'll stop asking your wretched questions? And you're never ever to tell Papa I showed you. He'd be very angry. Promise me now.'

"So I promised, promised faithfully, and then stood in their bedroom and watched as she climbed up on a chair to get it down from where it had been hidden on top of the cupboard. It was wrapped up in an old grey

blanket. I knelt on the bed beside her as she
pulled away the blanket and
opened the violin case.
I remember it smelt
musty. The maroon
lining inside was
faded and worn
to tatters. Mama
picked up the
violin with
infinite care,
reverently
almost. Then
she handed it
to me.

"I stroked the polished grain of the wood, which was the colour of honey, dark honey on the front, and golden honey underneath. I ran my fingers along the black pegs, the mottled bridge, the exquisitely carved scroll. It was so light to hold, I remember. I wondered at its fragile beauty. I knew at once that all the music in the world was hidden away inside this violin, yearning to come out. I longed to be the one to let it out, to rest it under my chin, to play the strings, to try the bow. I wanted there and then to bring it to life, to have it sing for me, to hear all the music we could make together. But when I asked if I could play it, Mama took sudden fright and said Papa might hear down below in the barber's shop, and he'd be furious with her for showing it to me; that he never wanted it to be played again. He hadn't so much as looked at it in years. When I asked why, she reminded me of my promise not to ask any more questions. She almost snatched the violin off me, laid it back in its case, wrapped it again in the blanket and put it back up on top of the cupboard.

"'You don't know it exists, Paolo. You never saw it, understand? And from now on I don't want to hear another word about it, all right? You promised me, Paolo.'

"I suppose seeing Papa's old violin, holding

it as I had, marvelling at it, must have satisfied my curiosity for a while, because I kept my promise. Then late one summer's evening I was lying half awake in my bed when I heard the sound of a violin. I thought Papa must have changed his mind and was playing again at last. But then I heard him and Mama talking in the kitchen below, and realized anyway that the music was coming from much further away.

"I listened at the window. I could hear it only intermittently

over the sound of people talking and walking, over the throbbing engines of passing water buses, but I was quite sure now that it was coming from somewhere beyond the bridge. I had to find out. In my pyjamas I stole past the kitchen door, down the stairs and out into the street. It was a warm night, and quite dark. I ran up over the bridge and there, all on his own, standing by the lamp in the square, was an old man playing the violin, his violin case open at his feet.

"No one else was there. No one had stopped to listen. I squatted down as close as I dared. He was so wrapped up in his playing that he did not notice me at first. I could see now that he was much older even than Papa. Then he saw me crouching there watching him. He stopped playing. 'Hello,' he said. 'You're out late. What's your name?' He had kind eyes; I noticed that at once.

"'Paolo,' I told him. 'Paolo Levi. My papa plays the violin. He played in an orchestra once.'

"'So did I,' said the old man, 'all my life. But now I am what I always wanted to be, a soloist. I shall play you some Mozart. Do you like Mozart?'

"'I don't know,' I replied. I knew Mozart's name, of course, but I don't think I had ever listened to any of his music.

"'He wrote this piece when he was even younger than you. I should guess that you're about seven.'

"'Nine,' I said.

"'Well, Mozart wrote this when he was just six years old. He wrote it for the piano, but I can play it on the violin.'

"So he played Mozart, and I listened. As he played, others came and gathered round for a while before dropping a coin or two in his violin case and moving on. I didn't move on. I stayed. The music he played to me that night touched my soul. It was the night that changed my life for ever.

"Whenever I crossed the Accademia

Bridge after that I always looked out for him. Whenever I heard him playing I went to listen. I never told Mama or Papa. I think it was the first secret I kept from them. But I did not feel guilty about it, not one bit. After all, hadn't they kept a secret from me? Then one evening the old man – I had found out by now that his name was Benjamin Horowitz and that he was sixty-two years old – one evening he let me hold his violin, showed me how to hold it properly, how to draw the bow across the strings, how to make it sing. The moment I did that, I knew I had to be a violinist. I have never wanted to do or be anything else since.

"So Benjamin – Signor Horowitz I always called him then – became my first teacher. Now every time I ran over the bridge to see him he would show me a little more, how to tighten the bow just right, how to use the resin, how to hold the violin under my chin using no hands at all and what each string was called. That was when I told him about Papa's violin at home, and about how he didn't play it any more. 'He couldn't anyway,' I said, 'because it's a bit broken. I think it needs mending a bit. Two of the strings are missing, the A and the E, and there's hardly a hair left on the bow at all. But I could practise on it if it was mended, couldn't I?'

"'Bring it to my house sometime,' Benjamin said, 'and leave it with me. I'll see what I can do.'

"It wasn't difficult to escape unnoticed. I just waited till after school. Mama was still at the laundry round the corner in Rio de le Romite, where she worked. Papa was downstairs with his customers. To reach the violin on top of the cupboard I had to put a suitcase on the chair and then climb up. It wasn't easy but I managed. I ran through the streets hugging it to me. From the Dorsoduro to the Arsenale where Benjamin lived is not that far if you know the way – nowhere is that far in Venice – and I knew the way quite well because my Aunt Sophia lived there and we visited her often. All I had to do was find Benjamin's street. I had to ask about a bit, but I found it.

"Benjamin lived up a narrow flight of stairs in one small room with a bed in one corner and a basin in the other. On the wall were lots of concert posters. 'Some of the concerts I played,' he said. 'Milan, London,

New York. Wonderful places, wonderful people, wonderful music. It is a wonderful world out there. There are times when it can be hard to go on believing that. But always believe it, Paolo, because it is true. And music helps to make it so. Now, show me that violin of yours.'

"He studied it closely, holding it up to the light, tapping it. 'A very fine instrument,' he said. 'You say this belongs to your father?'

"'And now I want to play it myself,' I told him.

"'It's a bit on the large side for a young lad like you,' he said, tucking the violin under my chin and stretching my arm to see how far I could reach. 'But a big violin is better than no violin at all. You'll manage. You'll grow into it.'

"'And when it's mended, will you teach me?' I asked him. 'I've got lots of money saved up from my sweeping; so many notes they cover all my bed when I spread them out, from the end of the bed right up to my pillow.'

"He laughed at that and told me he would teach me for nothing because I was his best listener, his lucky mascot. 'When you're not there,' he said, 'everyone walks by and my violin case stays empty. Then you come along and sit there. That's when they always stop to listen and that's when they leave their money. So a lesson or two will just be paying you back, Paolo. I'll have the violin ready as soon as I can and then we can start your lessons.'

"It was a week or two before the violin was mended. I dreaded that Mama or Papa might discover it was missing. But my luck held, and they didn't, and my lessons began. Whenever I wasn't having my lessons with Benjamin, Papa's violin, now restrung and restored, lay in its case wrapped in the grey blanket and hidden away on top of their bedroom cupboard.

My secret was safe, I thought. But secrets are never safe, however well hidden. Sooner or later truth will out, and in this case it was to be sooner rather than later.

"I took to the violin as if it had been a limb I had been missing all my life. I seemed to be able to pick up everything Benjamin taught me, effortlessly and instinctively. Under his kind tutelage my confidence simply burgeoned, my playing blossomed. I found I could make my violin – Papa's violin, rather – sing with the voice of an angel. Benjamin and I felt the excitement and pleasure of my progress as keenly as each other. 'I think this instrument was invented just for you, Paolo,' he told me one day. 'Or maybe you were made for it. Either way it is a perfect match.' I loved every precious moment of my lessons and always dreaded their ending. We would finish every lesson with a cup of mint tea made with fresh mint. I loved it. Ever since, I have always treated myself to a cup of mint tea after practice. It's something I always look forward to.

"I remember one day with the lesson over, we were drinking tea at his table when he looked across at me, suddenly very serious. 'It is strange, Paolo,' he said, 'but as I was watching you playing a moment ago, I felt I had known you before, a long, long time ago. And then just now I thought about your name, Levi. It is a common enough name, I know, but his name was Levi too. It is him you remind me of. I am sure of it. He was the youngest player in our orchestra, no more than a boy really. Gino, he was called.'

"'But my father is called Gino,' I told him. 'Maybe it was him. Maybe you played with my father. Maybe you know him.'

"'It can't be possible,' Benjamin breathed. He was staring at me now as if I were a ghost. 'No, it can't be. The Gino Levi I knew must be dead, I am sure of it. I have not heard of him in a long while, a very long while. But you never know, I suppose. Maybe I should meet your papa, and your mama too. It's about time anyway. You've been coming for lessons for over six months now. They need to know they have a wonderful violinist for a son.'

"'No, you can't!' I cried. 'He'd find out! You can't tell him. You mustn't!' Then I told him, through my tears, all my secret, about how Mama had shown me Papa's violin and made me promise never to say anything, never to tell Papa, and how I'd kept it a secret all this while: mending the violin, the lessons, everything.

"'Secrets, Paolo,' said Benjamin, 'are lies by another name. You do not lie to those you love. A son should not hide things from his papa and his mama. You must tell them your secret, Paolo. If you want to go on playing the violin, you will have to tell them. If you want me to go on teaching you, you will have to tell them. And now is usually a good time to do what must be done, particularly when you don't want to do it.'

"'Will you come with me?' I begged him. 'I can only do it if you come with me.'

"'If you like,' he said, smiling.

"Benjamin carried Papa's violin for me that day, and held my hand all the way back to the Dorsoduro. I dreaded having to make my confession. I knew how hurt they would be. All the way I rehearsed what I was going to say over and over again.

Mama and Papa were upstairs in the kitchen when we came in. I introduced Benjamin and then, before anyone had a chance to say anything, before I lost my courage entirely, I launched at once into my prepared confession, how I hadn't really stolen Papa's violin, just borrowed it to get it mended, and to practise on. But that's as far as I got. To my surprise they were not looking angry. In fact, they weren't looking at me at all. They were just staring up at Benjamin as if quite unable to speak. Benjamin spoke before they did. 'Your mama and papa and me, I think perhaps we do know one another,' he said. 'We played together once, did we not? Don't you remember me, Gino?'

"'Benjamin?' As Papa started to his feet, the chair went over behind him.

"'And if I am not much mistaken, Signora,' Benjamin went on, looking now at Mama, 'you must be little Laura Adler – all of us violins, all of us there, and all of us still here. It is like a miracle. It *is* a miracle.'

"What happened next I can see as if it were yesterday. It was suddenly as if I was not in the room at all. The three of them seemed to fill the kitchen, arms around each other, and crying openly, crying through their laughter. I stood there mystified, trying to piece together all I had heard, all that was going on before my eyes. Mama played the violin too! She had never told me that!

"'You see, Paolo,' said Benjamin, smiling down at me, 'didn't I tell you once it was a wonderful world? Twenty years. It's been twenty years or more since I last saw your mama and papa. I had no idea they were still alive. I always hoped they survived, hoped they were together, these two young lovebirds, but I never believed it, not really.'

"Mama was drying her eyes on her apron. Papa was so overcome, he couldn't speak. They sat down then, hands joined around the table as if unwilling to let each other go for fear this reunion might turn out to be no more than a dream.

"Benjamin was the first to recover. 'Paolo was about to tell you something, I think,' he said. 'Weren't you, Paolo?' I told them everything then: how I'd gone for my lessons, how Benjamin had been the best teacher in all the world. I dared to look up only when I'd finished. Instead of the disapproval and disappointment I had expected, both Mama and Papa were simply glowing with joy and pride.

"'Didn't I say Paolo would tell us, Papa?' Mama said. 'Didn't I tell you we should trust him? You see, Paolo, I often take down my violin, just to touch it, to look at it. Papa doesn't like me to, but I do it all the same, because this violin is my oldest friend. Papa forgives me, because he knows I love this violin, that it is a part of me. You remember I showed it to you that day, Paolo? It wasn't long after that it went missing, was it? I knew it had to be you. Then it came back, mended miraculously. And after school you were never home, and when you weren't home the violin was always gone too. I told Papa, didn't I, Papa? I told him you'd tell us when you were ready. We put two and two together; we thought you might be practising somewhere, but it never occurred to us that you were having lessons, nor that you had a teacher – and certainly not that your teacher was Benjamin Horowitz, who taught us and looked after us like a father all those years ago.' She cried again then, her head on Papa's shoulder.

"'But you told me it was Papa's violin, that he'd put it away and never wanted to play it again, ever,' I said.

"At this the three of them looked at one another. I knew then they all shared the same secret, and that without a word passing between them they were deciding whether they should reveal it, if this was the right moment to tell me. I often wondered later whether, if Benjamin had not come that day, they would ever have told me. As it was they looked to Papa for the final decision, and it was he who invited me to the table to join them. I think I knew then, even before Papa began, that I was in some way part of their secret.

"'Mama and me,' Papa began, 'we try never to speak of this, because the memories we have are like nightmares, and we want to forget. But you told us your secret. There is a time for truth, it seems, and it has come. Truth for truth, maybe.'

"So began the saddest, yet the happiest story I ever heard. When the story became too painful, as it often did, they passed it from one to the other, so that all three shared it. I listened horrified, at the same time honoured that they trusted me enough with their story, the story of their lives. Each told their part with great care, explaining as they went along so that I would understand, because I was a boy of nine who knew very little then of the wickedness of the world. I wish I could remember their exact words, but I can't, so I won't even try. I'll just tell you their story my own way, about how they lived together, how they nearly died together and how they were saved by music.

"The three of them were brought by train to the concentration camp from all over Europe: Benjamin from Paris, Mama from Warsaw, Papa from here, from Venice; all musicians, all Jewish, and all bound for the gas chamber and extermination like so many millions. They survived only because they were all able to say yes to one question put to them by an SS officer on arrival at the camp. 'Is there anyone amongst you who can play an orchestral instrument, who is a professional musician?' They did not know when they stepped forward that they would at once be separated from their familics, would have to watch them being herded off towards those hellish chimneys, never to be seen again.

"There were auditions, of course, and by now they knew they were playing for their lives. There were rehearsals then, and it was during these rehearsals that the three of them first met. Benjamin was a good twenty years older than Mama and Papa, who were very much the babies of the orchestra, both of them just twenty. Why the orchestra was rehearsing, who they would be playing for, they did not know and they did not ask. To ask was to draw attention to oneself. This, they knew, was not the way to survive, and in the camp to survive was everything. They played Mozart, a lot of Mozart. The repertoire was for the most part light and happy –

Eine kleine Nachtmusick,

the Clarinet Concerto in A major,

minuets, dances, marches. And Strauss

was popular too, waltzes, always waltzes.

Playing was very hard because their fingers

were so cold that sometimes they could hardly feel them, because they were weak with hunger and frequently sick. Sickness had to be hidden, because sickness, once discovered, would mean death. The SS were always there watching, and everyone knew too what awaited them if they did not play well enough.

"At first they gave concerts only for the SS officers. Papa said you just had to pretend they were not there. You simply lost yourself in the music – it was the only way. Even when they applauded you did not look up. You never looked them in the eye. You played with total commitment. Every performance was your best performance, not to please them, but to show them what you could do, to prove to them how good you were despite all they were doing to humiliate you, to destroy you in body and soul. 'We fought back with our music,' Papa said. 'It was our only weapon.'

"Papa could speak no Polish, Mama no Italian, but their eyes met as they were playing – as often as possible, Mama said. To begin with, it might have been their shared joy in music-making, but very soon they knew they loved one another. The whole orchestra knew it, even before they did, Benjamin told me.

'Our little lovebirds' they were called. For everyone else in the orchestra, he said, they represented a symbol of hope for the future; and so they were much loved, much protected.

For Mama and Papa their love numbed the pain and was a blessed refuge from the constant fear they were living through, from the horror of all that was going on around them.

"But there was amongst them a shared shame. They were being fed when others were not. They were being kept alive while others went to the gas chamber. Many were consumed by guilt, and this guilt was multiplied a thousand times when they discovered the real reason the orchestra had been assembled, why they had been rehearsing all this time. The concerts for the SS officers turned out to be sinister dress rehearsals for something a great deal worse.

"One cold morning with snow on the ground, they were made to assemble out in the compound with their instruments and ordered to sit down and play close to the camp gates. Then the train arrived, the wagons packed with new prisoners. Once they were all out they were lined up and then divided. The old and young and the frail were herded past the orchestra on their way, they were told, to the shower block; the able-bodied, those fit for work, were taken off towards the huts. And all the while Mama and Papa and Benjamin and the others played their Mozart. They all understood soon enough what it was for − to calm the terror, to

beguile each new trainload into a false sense of security. They were part of a deadly sham. They knew well enough that the shower block was a gas chamber.

"Week after week they played, month after month, train after train. And twenty-four hours a day the chimneys of the crematorium spewed out their fire and their smoke and their stench. Until there were no more trains; until the day the camps were liberated. This was the last day Benjamin ever remembered seeing Mama and Papa. They were all terribly emaciated by now, he said, and looked unlikely to survive. But they had. Mama and Papa had walked together out of the camp. They had played duets for bread and shelter, all across Europe. They were still playing to survive.

"When at last they got home to Venice, Papa smashed his violin and burned it, vowing never to play music again. But Mama kept hers. She thought of it as her talisman, her saviour and her friend, and she would neither sell it nor abandon it. She said it had brought her through all the horrors of the camp, brought them safely across Europe, back to Papa's home in Venice. It had saved their lives.

"Papa kept his vow. He never played a note of music again. After all that had happened he could hardly bear to hear it, which is why Mama had not played her violin either in all these years. But she would not be parted from it and had kept it safe at the top of their bedroom cupboard, hoping against hope, she said, that one day Papa might change his mind and be able to love music again and even play it. He never had. But they had survived and they were in time blessed with a child, a boy they called Paolo – a happy ending, Benjamin said. And I was the one who had brought the three of them together again, he said. So two happy endings.

"As for Benjamin, he had found his way back to Paris after a while, and played again in his old orchestra. He had married a French girl, Françoise, a cellist who had died only recently. He had come to Venice because he had always loved visiting the city and always longed to live looking out over water, and because Vivaldi was born here – he had always loved Vivaldi above all other composers. He played in the streets not just for the money, though that was a help, but because he could not bear not to play his violin. And he loved playing solo violin at last. He was more like Mama, he said. It was music that had kept him alive in the camp, and music had been his constant companion ever since. He could not imagine living a single day of his life without it, which was why, he said, he would dearly like to go on teaching me, if Mama and Papa would allow it.

"'Does he play well, Benjamin?' Mama asked. 'Can we hear him, Papa? Please.'

"Papa, I could see, was struggling with himself. 'So long as it's not Mozart,' he said finally. So I played the Winter movement from Vivaldi's *Four Seasons*, Benjamin's favourite piece. Papa sat listening with closed eyes throughout.

"When I had finished, Benjamin said, 'Well, Gino, what do you think? He has a

great and wonderful talent, your son, a rare gift you have both given him.'

"'Then it must not be wasted,' said Papa quietly.

"So every day without fail after that I went for my violin lessons with Benjamin in his little apartment in the Arsenale. Papa could not bring himself to listen to me playing, but sometimes Mama came along with me and sat and listened, and afterwards she always hugged me so tight it hurt; but I did not mind, not one bit. I began to play in the streets alongside Benjamin, and whenever I did the crowds became bigger and bigger each time. One day Papa was there amongst

them watching, listening. He walked me home afterwards, saying not a word until we were walking over the Accademia Bridge. 'So, Paolo,' he said, 'you prefer playing the violin to sweeping up in my barber's shop, do you?'

"'Yes, Papa,' I replied. 'I'm afraid I do.'

"'Well then, I can see I shall just have to do my sweeping up myself.' He stopped then and put his hands on my shoulders. 'I shall tell you something, Paolo, and I want you never to forget it. When you play I can listen to music again. You have made music joyful for me once more, and that is a wonderful gift you have given me. You go and be the

great violinist you should be. I shall help you all I can. You will play heavenly music and people will love you. Mama and I shall come to all your concerts, or as many as we can. But you have to promise me one thing: that until the day I die you will never play Mozart in public, not in my hearing. It was Mozart we played so often in the camp. Never Mozart. Promise me.'

"So I promised. I have kept my promise to Papa all these years. He died two weeks ago, the last of the three of them to go. At my fiftieth birthday concert in London I shall be playing Mozart, and I shall be playing it on Mama's violin, and I shall play it so well that he will love it, they will all love it, wherever they are."

I was still finishing my shorthand when I looked up and saw him coming towards me. He was offering me his violin.

"Here you are," he said. "Mama's violin. My violin. You can hold it if you like while we have some more mint tea. You'll have another cup, won't you? I make the best mint tea in Venice."

So I held Paolo Levi's violin for several precious minutes as we sat talking quietly over a last cup of tea. I asked him no more questions. There were none to ask. He talked of his love of Venice, and how wherever he was in the world he longed to be back home. It was the sounds he always missed: the church bells, the walking and talking, the chuntering of boats, and the music in the streets. "Music belongs in the streets, where Benjamin played it," he said, "not in concert halls."

As I left, he looked me in the eye and said, still grasping my hand, "I am glad it was you I told."

"Why did you?" I asked. "Why did you tell me?"

"Because it was time to tell the truth. Because secrets are lies, and because you have eyes that are kind, like Benjamin's. But mostly because you didn't ask the Mozart question."

"It is difficult for us to imagine how dreadful was the suffering that went on in the Nazi concentration camps during the Second World War. The enormity of the crime that the Nazis committed is just too overwhelming for us to comprehend. In their attempt to wipe out an entire race they caused the deaths of six million people, most of them Jews. It is when you hear the stories of the individuals who lived through it – Anne Frank, Primo Levi – that you can begin to understand the horror just a little better, and to understand the evil that caused it.

For me, the most haunting image does not come from literature or film, but from music. I learned some time ago that in many of the camps the Nazis selected Jewish prisoners and forced them to play in orchestras; for the musicians it was simply a way to survive. In order to calm the new arrivals at the camps they were made to serenade them as they were lined up and marched off, many to the gas chambers. Often they played Mozart.

I wondered how it must have been for a musician who played in such hellish circumstances, who adored Mozart as I do – what thoughts came when playing Mozart later in life. This was the genesis of my story, this and the sight of a small boy in a square by the Accademia Bridge in Venice, sitting one night, in his pyjamas on his tricycle, listening to a busker. He sat totally enthralled by the music that seemed to him, and to me, to be heavenly."

Michael Morpurgo

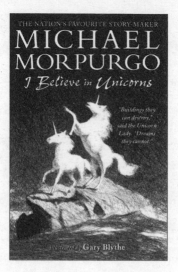

Eight-year-old Tomas hates school,
hates books and hates stories. Forced to visit
the library, he stops to listen to the magical
tales that the Unicorn Lady spins – tales
that draw him in, making themselves part
of him and changing the course of
his life for ever.

MICHAEL
MORPURGO
THE KITES ARE FLYING!
ILLUSTRATED BY LAURA CARLIN

FRIENDSHIP KNOWS NO BARRIERS

Journalist Max and his new friend Said sit
together under an ancient olive tree while
Said makes another of his kites. Max is
welcomed as a guest in the boy's home, and
learns of the terrible events in his family's
past – but nothing prepares him for the true
importance of Said's kites. A beautiful tale
of tragedy and hope that rings with joy.

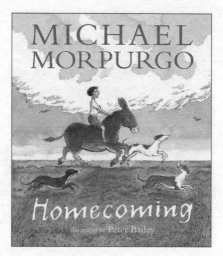

Michael loves to visit Mrs Pettigrew in her railway carriage by the sea, where she lives with her donkey, dogs and hens. But when plans are made to build a nuclear power station, Mrs Pettigrew's idyllic life becomes threatened and Michael learns that nothing can ever stay the same.

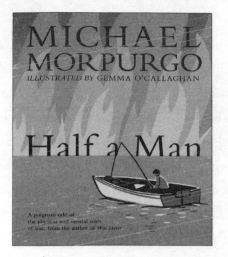

Michael is fascinated by and afraid of his grandfather in equal measure, with his disfigured, unsmiling face and taciturn manner. Then a summer spent on the Isles of Scilly enables him to finally see the man behind the burns – and gives Michael the power to heal wounds that have divided his family for so long.

Michael Morpurgo was 2003–2005 Children's Laureate, has written over one hundred books and is the winner of numerous awards, including the Whitbread Children's Book Award, the Blue Peter Book Award, the Smarties Book Prize and the Red House Children's Book Award. His books are translated and read around the world and his hugely popular novel *War Horse*, already a critically acclaimed stage play, is now also a blockbuster film. Michael and his wife, Clare, founded the charity Farms for City Children and live in Devon.

Michael Foreman is one of the world's leading illustrators. He has won several major awards, including the Smarties Prize, the Kate Greenaway Medal (twice), the Francis Williams Prize (twice) and the *Aigle d'Argent* at the *Festival International du Livre* in France. He is the illustrator of *Beowulf* and *Sir Gawain and the Green Knight* by Michael Morpurgo, as well as classics such as *War Boy*, *Mia's Story*, *Say Hello* and *A Child's Garden*. He lives in south-west London.